Dark Tricks

To Tabitha Fox-Jalland, who would probably have
at least ten Star Animals (including a Star Sheep)
following her around!—L.C.

To Katherine—L.F.

tiger tales

5 River Road, Suite 128, Wilton, CT 06897
Published in the United States 2020
Originally published in Great Britain 2018
by the Little Tiger Group
Text copyright © 2018 Linda Chapman
Illustrations copyright © 2018 Lucy Fleming
ISBN-13: 978-1-68010-469-1
ISBN-10: 1-68010-469-1
Printed in the USA
STP/4800/0380/0920
2 4 6 8 10 9 7 5 3

For more insight and activities,
visit us at www.tigertalesbooks.com

Star Friends
Dark Tricks

BY LINDA CHAPMAN

ILLUSTRATED BY LUCY FLEMING

tiger tales

Contents

1

IN THE STAR WORLD

A waterfall of stars fell into a beautiful pool. A snowy owl and a silver wolf stood beside it, watching intently as an image appeared in the water—a gray-haired lady holding a glittering black stone.

"I don't like this, Hunter," the wolf said. "She is full of bitterness and jealousy, and she is planning on harming the new Star Friends."

The owl nodded in concern and swept his wing across the surface of the water. The image of the elderly lady dissolved and reformed, this time showing four ten-year-old girls chatting in a bedroom. There were four animals with them—a fox, a wildcat, a young deer, and a red squirrel. Each of the animals had unusual indigo eyes—they were animals from the Star World.

The wolf gazed at one of the girls—she had shoulder-length, dark blond hair and determined eyes. The fox was cuddled up next to her, resting his head on her shoulder. "Mia looks so much like her grandmother," the wolf said.

"I hope she has her grandmother's courage and cleverness," said the owl gravely. "These four girls and their Star Animals will have to be very brave if they are going to stop the one using dark magic. They will have to trust their instincts, their friendship—but most of all, their hearts…."

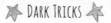

2
A LITTLE MORNING MAGIC

Mia Greene sat cross-legged on her bed. Magic tingled through her, making her feel as if every inch of her skin was sparkling. Her Star Animal, Bracken the fox, sat beside her, but her eyes were fixed on the small mirror in her hands. Through her bedroom door, she could hear her older sister, Cleo, shouting to their mom that she couldn't find her favorite skirt.

"Show me where Cleo's favorite skirt is," Mia whispered.

The surface of the mirror shimmered, and

a picture appeared. It showed a red skirt lying in a pile underneath the dresser in Cleo's bedroom.

"Found it!" Mia said in delight. When she had first started learning how to do magic, it would take her quite a while to connect with the magic current, but now she could do it almost instantly.

Mia had been able to use magic ever since Bracken and some other animals from the Star World had appeared to find Star Friends. Only those who truly believed in magic could hear the Star Animals speaking. Together, a Star Friend and their Star Animal would use the magical current that flowed between the two worlds to help people. Each Star Friend had different magical abilities, and when they used magic for good, it strengthened the current.

Bracken nuzzled Mia, his soft fur tickling her skin. "You're getting so good at using magic!"

he said.

Mia breathed in his familiar sweet scent—the smell of grass in the woods on a warm autumn day. "Good. I need to be strong if we want to stop whoever is using dark magic. We all need to be."

Mia's three best friends, Lexi, Sita, and Violet, were also Star Friends. Together they had discovered that someone nearby was using dark magic to conjure Shades, and that this was weakening the magical current. Shades were evil spirits who brought misery and unhappiness into people's lives, and Star Friends could use their magic to send them back to the shadows.

"We'll find whoever is conjuring Shades and stop them," Bracken declared. "Are we meeting up with the others today?"

"Yes, we're going to Violet's house later this morning. I thought I'd stop by Aunt Carol's on the way."

Aunt Carol had been friends with Mia's grandmother before she had died. She was the only adult Mia knew who could do magic— she wasn't a Star Friend like Mia, but used crystals and stones.

Mia heard her sister shouting on the landing again. "Oops, I still haven't told Cleo where her skirt is."

Bracken disappeared in a shimmer of starlight as Mia opened the bedroom door. None of Mia's family knew about him—the Star World had to be kept secret from people who didn't believe in magic.

Cleo was standing at the top of the stairs shouting, "I've looked *everywhere!*"

"Wear something else, then," her mom said.

"But I want to wear my skirt!"

Mia went into Cleo's messy bedroom and hurried over to the dresser. She crouched down. Just then, Cleo came into the room. "What are you doing in here?" she asked.

"I thought I'd help you look for your skirt," said Mia. "Is this it?" She pulled the red skirt out from under the dresser.

"Yes!" Cleo gasped. She frowned. "Did you put it there?"

"No!" Mia protested. "Just a lucky guess."

Their mom appeared in the doorway. "Cleo, this room is a mess. It's no wonder you can't find anything!"

"Mom! Mia found my skirt!" Cleo said. "You keep doing this—finding things that are lost. How do you do it?"

Mia hid her smile. If only Cleo knew the truth! "I guess I'm just good at finding things."

"I think you're psychic," said Cleo, staring at her. "You should start a social media channel!"

Mia laughed it off but thought that maybe she should be a little more careful about how she used her magic from now on.

"Cleo, I hardly think Mia's psychic," Mom said, smiling. "I think you're just very bad at looking. Now get changed quickly, and I'll drop you off at your friend's house. What are you going to do this morning, Mia?" she asked as they both left Cleo's room.

"I'm meeting the others at Violet's house. Is it okay if I go to Aunt Carol's on the way?"

"Of course," Mom said. "Aunt Carol always loves to see you. Tell her I'll stop by for a cup of tea soon."

"Okay," Mia said, and she hurried down the stairs.

3
A VISIT WITH AUNT CAROL

As Mia rode her bike through the streets of Westport, the coastal town where she lived, the frosty November air stung her cheeks. Autumn had definitely turned to winter now—the branches of the trees were almost bare, and there was a thin coating of frost on the grass.

As she rode along, the locals she passed smiled at her and said hello. It was hard to believe that someone in town wanted to use magic to hurt people. But Mia and her friends had dealt with a Mirror Shade who had been

making Cleo jealous of her best friend and a
Wish Shade trapped inside a garden gnome
who had made a little girl's wish come true in
horrible ways. Then, last week, they had faced
Fear Shades that were hidden in four little
yellow stretchy men. The Fear Shades had made
it seem as if people's worst fears were coming
true. Luckily, Mia and her friends had realized
what was going on and had managed to send
them back to the shadows, too.

We have to find out who is causing all this
trouble, Mia thought.

Mia got off her bike and leaned it against
the wall in front of Aunt Carol's house. She
glanced toward the house on the right, feeling
guilty as she remembered how she and the
others had suspected that the eccentric elderly
lady who lived there—Mrs. Crooks—was the
person doing dark magic. The Wish Shade
in the gnome had told them that the person
who had conjured him was a woman, and

when they had first met Mrs. Crooks, they
had suspected her right away. She liked to
go out into the woods at night, she was very
grumpy, she had a bunch of garden gnomes,
and Sorrel had even smelled Shades near her
yard. But it had turned out that Mrs. Crooks
was just a harmless elderly lady who didn't like
children very much and loved to collect garden
ornaments and rescue injured animals in the
woods.

Looking at the two gnomes sitting on either
side of Mrs. Crooks' front door, Mia wondered
who had put the Wish Shade in the gnome that
had been given to Paige.

Aunt Carol opened her front door and beamed. "Hello, Mia. I wasn't expecting you."

"I was on my way to Violet's, and I thought I'd stop in," said Mia.

"How lovely! I've just made some of my chocolate cookies—the ones I know you like."

Mia took off her shoes in the hall and went through to the familiar living room, with its displays of polished stones and crystals decorating the shelves. She spotted an open cardboard box filled with cute knitted Christmas decorations on the coffee table— there were penguins, snowmen, and reindeer, all with beautiful sparkling eyes made out of tiny black crystals.

"These are beautiful," Mia said to Aunt Carol.

"Thank you, Mia. I've been making them to sell at the Christmas fair this weekend. You are going to come, aren't you?"

The Christmas fair was held every November

in the town hall. There were homemade cakes for sale as well as Christmas decorations, cards, and gifts. Mia's Grandma Anne had organized it when she was alive, and Mia had been to it every year for as long as she could remember.

"Yes, I'll be there," Mia said.

"It'll be strange without your grandma this year," said Aunt Carol. "But we'll make sure it's a really special one. The town will have the fair it deserves! Now come into the kitchen and have a cookie."

They went into the kitchen at the back of the house and sat down at the table. "Have you and your friends gotten any closer to solving the mystery of who is conjuring the Shades?" Aunt Carol asked as Mia helped herself to a cookie. "When I last saw you, you said that you thought it might be Mrs. Crooks. I've been keeping an eye on her, and she does act suspiciously—going out into the woods at all times of the day and night and—"

"Oh, it's okay, Aunt Carol," Mia put in. "It's not Mrs. Crooks. We still don't know who it is, though. But we think that whoever it is put stretchy men with Shades trapped inside them onto the boxes of sparklers you gave us."

Aunt Carol looked shocked. "Those little stretchy men had Shades in them?"

Mia nodded and gave a shiver. "Yes. Fear Shades. They were horrible."

"But you've sent them back to the Shadows? How did you manage that?" said Aunt Carol, intrigued.

"It was Violet and Sita, really," said Mia. "Violet's a Spirit Speaker, so she sent them back to the shadows, and Sita discovered she has this amazing ability—she can use her magic to command people and spirits to do what she wants. If she orders you to do something, you have to do it."

"Really?" Aunt Carol breathed. "That's a very rare ability. Your grandmother had it, too."

Mia nodded. She'd used her magic to look back into the past and had seen her grandmother using the same powers as Sita. Star Friends all had different magical abilities— Mia could use the magic current to see into the past and future and to see things that were happening elsewhere. Lexi could become very agile and fast, and Violet could travel from place to place using shadows and command Shades to return to the shadows as well as casting illusions. At first, they'd thought that Sita's magic just allowed her to heal and soothe. But then, last week, she had discovered she could command people and spirits, too. "I don't think Sita likes being so powerful."

"Well, if she wants to talk about it, she's always welcome here," said Aunt Carol. "I might be able to help."

"Thanks, I'll tell her," Mia said. Suddenly, she remembered something she'd been meaning to ask. "Where did you get those sparklers from,

Aunt Carol? The ones that the stretchy men were attached to?"

"From the garden center," said Aunt Carol. "If I'd known there were Shades in those stretchy men, I never would have given them to you. I wonder who put them there. Have you tried using the Seeing Stone to find out?"

"No, but I have been using it to look at other things," said Mia. Aunt Carol had given Mia a pale pink Seeing Stone to help her look into the past. Although Mia could use Star Magic to do that, she found it much easier with the Seeing Stone. "I've been looking into the past, to when you and Grandma Anne were younger. I've seen you doing magic together."

"I'm glad you've been using it." Aunt Carol smiled. "You're a natural with crystal magic as well as Star Magic."

Mia glowed proudly. "I'd better go," she said, checking the clock on the wall, "or the others will wonder where I am."

"Wait a minute." Aunt Carol hurried to the living room and came back with four knitted decorations. "Please give one to each of your friends to say how sorry I am about those stretchy men."

"Thank you," said Mia.

As she headed to the front door, she noticed a large snow globe on the side table in the hallway. She was surprised to see that it was empty except for a thin layer of snow. "I've never seen a snow globe without anything inside it before," she said.

"It won't be empty for long. This is going to be a very special snow globe," said Aunt Carol.

"Why?" asked Mia curiously.

"Oh, you'll find out," Aunt Carol said, tapping her nose. "I just need to test it first." Mia opened her mouth, but Aunt Carol said, "Now don't ask any questions. Like I said, you'll find out soon enough."

Mia put on her coat and helmet and rode off as Aunt Carol waved from the doorway. What had Aunt Carol meant? *Maybe the snow globe is magic and she's going to put something special inside it as a present*, Mia thought excitedly.

Crossing the main road, she turned onto the road that led down to the beach. Seeing Lexi and Sita arriving at the driveway of Violet's house, Mia rode quickly to catch up with her friends.

4
A Star Friends Meeting

"Hi, Mia!" Lexi called, jumping off her bike. Her black curls stuck out from under her pink helmet. She pulled it off and readjusted the butterfly clip in her hair.

"Hello." Sita's gentle brown eyes sparkled as she whispered, "Are you ready to do magic?"

Mia grinned. "Always."

As Mia propped her bike against the fence, she accidentally brushed her hand against some nettles. "Ow!" she exclaimed.

"Let me look," said Sita.

Mia held out her hand. Sita touched the nettle rash and concentrated for a second. The pain and tingling faded, and the bumps disappeared.

"That's awesome," said Mia, inspecting her hand. "Thank you."

Sita sighed happily. "I love using magic to heal."

The door opened, and Violet looked out. "I thought I heard you. Come in!" They all hurried upstairs to Violet's bedroom. As soon as the door was shut behind them, they called their Star Animals' names.

"Bracken!"

"Juniper!"

"Sorrel!"

"Willow!"

In a wave of starry light, the four animals appeared. Bracken put his paws up on Mia's knees and licked her face. Juniper, a red squirrel with a bushy tail, jumped onto the dressing table and then from there onto Lexi's shoulder. He tickled Lexi's cheek with his little paws, making her giggle and squirm. Willow, a deer with a coat the color of a chestnut, nuzzled Sita's hands, and Sorrel the wildcat wound through Violet's legs purring happily, her tail high in the air.

When the greetings were over, they all sat down on the rug, the animals happily cuddling up to their Star Friends.

"Has anyone used their magic since yesterday?" Mia asked.

"I have," said Lexi. "I was walking home from my piano lesson, and I saw a cat about to run into the road. I used my magic to move really quickly, and I grabbed it and took it to safety."

"That's amazing!" said Sita. "I used my magic to heal my baby brother after he bumped his head on the coffee table."

"Cool!" said Mia.

"Have you used your powers to command people yet?" Violet asked Sita.

Sita shook her head.

"I'd use that power if I had it," said Violet longingly.

"Why haven't you?" Lexi asked.

"I just haven't," Sita muttered.

Willow spoke up. "What have you used your magic for, Violet?"

"Violet's been wonderful," said Sorrel smugly. "Tell them, Violet."

"I used my magic to shadow-travel to the park. We'd been playing there, and my little cousin had left her cuddly monkey. I went to find it and bring it back," said Violet.

"Very clever," Sorrel said approvingly.

Mia caught sight of Lexi rolling her eyes. Sorrel always acted as if Violet was better than the rest of them. Mia didn't mind, but it irritated Lexi.

"How about you, Mia?" said Sita.

"Well, I used my magic to find Cleo's skirt this morning," Mia said.

"That's all you've done?" Sorrel said, not sounding impressed.

Bracken stiffened. "It might have been a small thing, but it was still a good deed." He rubbed his head against Mia's leg.

Sorrel gave him a cool look. "Not like Violet's."

"I bet Cleo was happy, though," said Violet quickly.

"Yes, but the trouble is, now she thinks I'm some kind of weird psychic," said Mia.

"Mystic Mia," Lexi said, grinning. "You could use your powers to tell people's fortunes and earn a lot of money."

Sorrel sniffed. "Do I need to remind you that magic should only be used for good?"

"Mia would be doing good—she'd be helping us!" said Lexi.

Juniper chattered as if he was laughing, and Bracken yapped playfully, but Sorrel flicked her tail around her paws, a disapproving look on her face.

"Have you been practicing looking into the past, Mia?" Sita asked.

"A bit," said Mia. She didn't want to admit she'd been using the Seeing Stone. Bracken

thought she should only use Star Magic, and
she had a feeling that the other Star Animals—
especially Sorrel—would agree with him.
"Oh, I just remembered something," she said,
changing the subject. "I stopped by to see
Aunt Carol on the way here, and she gave me
Christmas decorations for all of us." She took
them from her pocket and handed them out,
keeping a snowman for herself.

"Cute!" said Lexi, looking at her reindeer.

Sita looked at the penguin Mia had given
her. "My grandma would love this. She adores
penguins. I'll give it to her."

"Wait!" Sorrel hissed suddenly, her fur standing up. "Those decorations could have Shades in them." She pounced on the knitted snowman Violet was holding and sniffed it suspiciously. "They're safe," she said grudgingly.

"Of course they are," said Mia as Violet put the snowman on her desk. "Aunt Carol's decorations wouldn't be bad. She only uses magic for good."

"She did give you the stretchy men," Sorrel reminded them.

"But she hadn't even noticed them. She picked the boxes up from the garden center!" Mia protested.

Violet looked thoughtful. "Maybe if we go there, we might find out something about them."

"How do we get there, though?" said Lexi. "We could ask one of our parents to take us…."

"I could shadow-travel us!" exclaimed Violet. Recently, she had found out that she could take other people with her when she was shadow-traveling. She jumped to her feet. "Come on!"

"Wait! What if your mom comes in and sees that we're all gone?" said Sita.

"She'll be really worried," Willow added.

"I don't mind staying," offered Sita. "If your mom does pop in, I can say the rest of you went outside or something."

"I'll stay, too," Mia said. She wanted a chance to talk to Sita about her new powers. "I will use my magic so Sita and I can watch what you're doing," she told Lexi and Violet.

Violet looked at Lexi. "Okay, I guess it's you and me, then." She and Lexi had never been very good friends—they were both clever and very competitive—and they rarely did anything just the two of them.

"I guess it is," said Lexi, giving Mia a slightly panicked look.

Violet walked to a patch of shadows in the corner of the room and held out her hand. Lexi joined her—then they and their Star Animals disappeared.

5
GATHERING CLUES

Mia and Sita stared at the empty shadows.

"I hope they're okay," said Sita anxiously. "What if someone notices them suddenly appearing in the garden center?"

Mia pulled a small mirror out of her pocket—she always carried it with her in case she wanted to do magic. She said Lexi and Violet's names, and she saw in the mirror her friends stepping out of the shadows beside a display of lawnmowers. Luckily, no one seemed to notice. "They just got there. They seem okay.

I'll check again in a minute." She lowered the mirror. "So how are you?"

"Me? All right." Sita shrugged, tucking a strand of hair behind her ear. "Why?"

"I just wondered how you were feeling about being able to command people," Mia said.

Willow nudged Sita encouragingly. "Talk to Mia. Tell her."

"Well, to be honest, I… I don't like it," Sita muttered. "I'm not even sure if it's real. I mean, it could just have been a fluke when I stopped those stretchy men."

"It wasn't," Bracken said.

"No way," said Mia, shaking her head. "You told us to freeze, and none of us could move until you freed us. Your power's real."

"But it can't be!" Sita said desperately. "I can't even decide what clothes to wear in the morning or how to do my hair. I *can't* be the powerful one."

"But you are," Bracken told her. "And that's good, isn't it?"

"No. It's a mistake," Sita said. Her eyes filled with tears.

"Hey, don't stress about it," Mia said, squeezing Sita's hand. "Aunt Carol suggested that you stop over and see her if you want to talk. My grandma had the same power as you, and Aunt Carol can help you." Not wanting to upset Sita anymore, she changed the subject. "Should we check on the others again?"

This time, when Mia picked up the mirror, she saw Lexi and Violet standing by a display of gnomes. "They're by some garden gnomes!" she exclaimed. "They look just like the one the Wish Shade was in. Maybe he came from that garden center, just like the stretchy men!" Letting everything else fade away, she focused on the picture and heard Violet speak.

"Let's ask about them," she was
whispering to Lexi. "Then
we'll see if we can find
out more about the
stretchy men later."
She headed over
to a nearby store
assistant.

"Excuse me,
how much are the
gnomes?" Violet asked
politely.

The lady smiled. "They're
all different prices. The price tags are
underneath them. They're sweet, aren't they?"

Violet nodded. "Have they just arrived, or
have you had them for a while?"

"They came in a few months ago now."

"I think my grandma's friend might have
bought one," said Lexi, joining Violet. "It was a
gnome with a four-leaf clover on his hat. Does

that sound familiar?"

"Oh, yes! He was very cute," said the assistant. "He had a message on the base. *Make a Wish*, I think it said."

Lexi nodded fast. "That's the one."

"Do you remember when he was sold?" Violet asked eagerly.

The assistant nodded. "I do. It was about a month ago—and I remember the lady who bought him. She comes in quite a lot. She lives in Westport. Cheerful lady, small with gray hair and very blue eyes."

Mia's heart thumped. They had a description of the person who had bought the gnome!

"What's your grandma's friend's name?" the assistant asked

"Umm, she's…." Lexi gave Violet a panicked look. "She's…."

"Oh, my phone!" said Violet, pulling her phone out of her pocket. "It's my mom," she said to the assistant apologetically. "She's

probably wondering where we are. Thanks for
your help." She held up the phone to her ear.
"Hi, Mom," she said, pretending to answer a
call as she dragged Lexi away around the side
of a display of toys. "Yes, we're coming in just a
minute."

Lexi squeaked and pointed at a shelf where
there was a big box of stretchy men.

"Stretchy men!" Violet gasped. "I wonder
if these have Shades in them, too. Sorrel, come
here!" she whispered.

Mia caught her breath as she saw the wildcat
appear. What if someone spotted her?

Violet pushed a stretchy man toward the cat.
"Does this have a Shade in it?"

Sorrel sniffed. "No."

"Violet! Someone's coming. Quick!" Lexi
hissed.

"Time to go!" said Violet, throwing the
stretchy man back in the box.

Sorrel vanished, and Violet grabbed Lexi's

hand and pulled her into a patch of shadows.
They disappeared.

A second later, they were back in Violet's
bedroom, giggling and stumbling out of
the shadows beside Violet's closet. "Oh, my
goodness! Shadow-traveling is fun!" said Lexi.

"It really is, isn't it?" Violet gasped.

"What happened?" said Sita.

Lexi and Violet called Juniper and Sorrel's names, and the two animals appeared. Then they told the others what had happened.

"You both did exceptionally well," purred Sorrel.

Lexi grinned. "I didn't know what to say when the assistant asked me what my grandma's friend's name was. That was quick-thinking with the phone excuse, Violet."

Violet looked happy. "Thanks. Your idea of pretending your grandma's friend had bought a gnome was great, too. At least we know what the person who bought the gnome looks like now."

"She has gray hair and blue eyes, and she's small and from Westport," said Lexi.

They beamed at each other. Mia blinked. She didn't think she'd ever seen Lexi and Violet act like they were good friends before.

"There are quite a few older ladies in Westport like that," said Sita.

"I've got an idea," said Violet suddenly.
"All the elderly ladies are bound to go to
the Christmas fair this weekend. We can
make a list of everyone there who matches
that description. Then we can spy on them
using Mia's magic and see if any of them acts
suspiciously."

"That's a great plan!" said Mia. "I think
we've got some real clues to go on now." She
held out her hand. "Go us!"

"Go us!" echoed Sita, Violet, and Lexi, high-
fiving each other.

6
MIA'S BAD MOOD

When Mia got home, she hung her snowman decoration on the handle of her closet door. As she called Bracken, she picked up the Seeing Stone from her desk. It glowed with a faint golden light. "I might try using the Seeing Stone to see Grandma Anne and Aunt Carol in the past," she told Bracken. She loved watching her grandmother when she was younger.

Bracken scratched his nose with a paw. "You're a Star Friend—you should use Star Magic, not Crystal Magic."

Mia reluctantly put the Seeing Stone into her pocket and sat down in front of the mirror on her desk. "Show me Grandma Anne when she was just learning about being a Star Friend."

The surface of the mirror began to swirl. She waited for it to form a clear image, but all she caught were brief pictures that appeared and then vanished—a young Grandma Anne cuddling her silver wolf…Grandma Anne with her hand on the wolf's back, smiling happily… Grandma Anne arguing with someone…. Mia squinted, trying to see who it was. It looked like it could be Aunt Carol, but before Mia could decide, the image flickered and was replaced by Grandma Anne healing a horse's leg.

"What can you see?" Bracken asked.

"Just a lot of different images flashing by," said Mia in frustration. "My magic is not working correctly."

Bracken looked surprised. "It was working fine earlier. Try looking at something that's happening now."

Mia looked into the mirror again. "Show me … Aunt Carol."

The surface swirled again, and she caught a glimpse of Aunt Carol holding the snow globe. She was smiling … but then the image swirled away.

"Aunt Carol," Mia said again, but nothing happened. "I can't even look into the present right now!" Mia gave Bracken a confused glance. "What's going on?"

Bracken looked puzzled. "It's very strange. Maybe you should take a break and try again later."

But that night, Mia still couldn't see anything clearly. In the end, she gave up and fell asleep with Bracken in her arms.

✹ ✹ ✹

Mia woke up in a bad mood. It was a drizzly, gray morning, and on the way to school, Alex kept insisting that their mom stop the stroller so he could look at things.

"Cat!" he said. "Black cat."

"Yes, sweetie, that's right—it's a black cat," their mom said.

"Red car!" he said pointing to a shiny red car parked by the sidewalk. "Wanna see!"

Mrs. Greene pushed him over to it.

Mia felt irritation rise up inside her. "We're going to be late, Mom!"

"No, we're not," her mom said. "He just wants to take a look."

"He took a look!" said Mia.

Her mom frowned. "What's up with you this morning?"

"Nothing," Mia muttered.

"Dog!" said Alex next, pointing up ahead to where a brown and white spaniel was sniffing at some grass. The owner, Mrs. Patel, who had been a friend of Grandma Anne's, was talking to Aunt Carol.

Mia's mom went over to say hello.

"Hello, Mia. Hello, Alex," said Aunt Carol. "Off to school and playgroup?"

Mia forced herself to smile despite her bad mood. "Yep."

The dog licked Alex's outstretched hand and stuck her nose in his face. Alex giggled.

Mia crouched down to rub the dog's ears. Grandma Anne had sometimes taken care of Holly for the Patels when they went on vacation. "Hello, Holly dog," she said.

Holly bounced around Mia, her tail wagging really quickly.

"She's ready for her morning run in the woods," said Mrs. Patel. "Anytime you feel like dog-walking, Mia, feel free to come by!"

"I will," Mia promised.

She spotted Lexi, Sita, and Violet walking together a bit farther up the road. "I'll catch up with the others," she told her mom.

"All right. Have a good day!" her mom called.

Mia hurried after her friends. Sita looked lost in her thoughts, her hands playing with the ends of her blue and white polka-dot scarf, while Lexi and Violet were talking about the school math club, complaining about how the games and worksheets were always too easy. Mia felt a flicker of jealousy as she saw Lexi and Violet swap smiles, and she tried to push the feeling away. It was silly to be jealous—after all, she had been wanting Lexi and Violet to get along better for a long time.

They all greeted her. "Are we going to meet

after school so we can talk about stuff?" Violet
said as they went onto the playground.

"Yeah, and do *stuff*," said Lexi, raising her
eyebrows meaningfully. They tried not to
mention magic when there were other people
around, just in case anyone overheard.

"It's getting dark so early that we probably
won't be allowed to go to the clearing in the
woods," Violet said. "I'll ask if you can come
to my house."

"That's a good idea," said Sita.

"I guess," said Mia a bit grumpily. She saw
her friends give her surprised looks. "We went
to Violet's last time."

"We can go to yours if you want," said Violet.

"No, it's okay," said Mia. She put down her
bag and it fell over, spilling her books and
lunch onto the wet ground.

"Rotten bag," she said angrily as the others
helped her pick up her things, and she shoved
everything back in.

The bell rang, and they made their way over
to line up in their class groups. Lexi and Sita
were together in one fifth-grade class, and Mia
and Violet were in the other.

"Are you okay?" Violet said, falling into step
with Mia. "You seem like you're in a bad mood."

"I'm fine," snapped Mia.

Violet stared at her. "There's no need to bite
my head off!"

As the day went on, Mia's bad mood faded.
At the end of school, their parents agreed that
they could all go over to Violet's house. They
were walking along the road when Mia spotted
a notice on a lamppost with a photograph
of a brown and white dog. She frowned and

hurried over. "Look! The Patels' dog is missing. I just saw her this morning!" She read the notice.

MISSING! PLEASE HELP!

Holly, our springer spaniel, ran off during her morning walk in the woods and hasn't been seen since. If anyone finds her or sees her, please contact us right away.

Call Kavita Patel—555-6693

"I wonder what happened to her," Mia said.

"I hope she hasn't been run over," said Sita anxiously.

"Maybe we can help find her," said Violet. "*With magic*," she mouthed, glancing back to where her dad was walking along talking to another dad.

They all nodded and hurried on down the road.

7
SOMETHING STRANGE

Violet dumped her bag on her desk next to her snowman decoration. "I've got to find a place to put this," she said, holding it up.

"You could hang it from your mirror," suggested Lexi.

"I gave mine to my grandma yesterday," said Sita. "She really liked it. She's going to buy some more at the Christmas fair."

Violet shut the door. "Okay, let's call the animals and see if we can help find Holly."

The others nodded. As soon as the Star

Animals appeared and heard about the missing dog, they agreed that the girls should try and find her using magic.

"Whose magic should we use?" Lexi asked.

"Well, I think it's obvious," said Violet. "We use Mia's magic to see where the dog is, and then you and I will shadow-travel there. If it's trapped somewhere, you can use your agility to rescue it. All set!"

Mia bit her lip. Her bad mood felt like it was creeping back. Why did Violet always think her plans were the best? "What about Sita?" she said. "That means she doesn't do anything."

"Maybe not everyone's magic is needed this time, Mia," Bracken said.

Annoyance flashed through Mia. "I think we should try and use everyone's magic."

"Why are you being so difficult?" Violet said.

"Yeah, Mia, what's your problem?" Lexi asked, frowning.

Mia glared. They were all ganging up on her!

"I don't mind if I'm not needed," Sita said quickly. "If the dog is injured or needs calming down, I can help in that way." She squeezed Mia's hand. "Thanks for being a good friend, though."

Mia felt the tension inside her slowly drain away. She started to sigh in relief, but then she realized what Sita was doing. "You're using your magic on me!" she exclaimed indignantly.

"No! Well, not my commanding magic. It's only my soothing, healing magic," Sita said. "I was just trying to help—you seemed tense."

"I'm not tense!" Mia exclaimed. She saw her

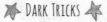

friends and their animals exchange surprised looks and added, "Oh, this is ridiculous! You can all find Holly without me!"

"Mia!" Bracken raced up and put his paws on her knees. "This isn't like you. What's the matter?"

Mia took a deep breath and crouched down, burying her face in his fur. Breathing in his familiar scent, she felt her anger begin to fade. "I'm sorry," she said, looking up at the others. "I don't know why I'm in such a bad mood."

"Hey, let's concentrate on trying to find Holly," said Sita. "Doing magic and helping people always makes us feel happy."

Bracken nuzzled Mia's cheek. "Can you use your mirror to try and find the dog?"

Mia nodded. She pulled the mirror out of her pocket and held it in front of her. "Holly, the Patels' dog," she told it, opening herself to the magical current. She felt it flow through her like a stream of glittering light, chasing away every

drop of irritation and tension.
At first, all she saw in the
mirror was whiteness,
but then an image of
the brown and white
spaniel appeared.
Where was she?

Mia looked more
closely, searching
for clues. Everywhere
around Holly was just
white. Suddenly, Mia realized
it was snow!

"What are you seeing?" Bracken asked her.

"Snow," she said, feeling puzzled. "But that
can't be right." She glanced out the window and
saw drizzle falling from the gray sky. There was
definitely no snow. She tried again. "Show me
where Holly, the Patels' dog, is." But the image
didn't change. "I don't know what to do. My
magic isn't showing me where she is."

"Don't worry," said Willow. "Bracken, Juniper, Sorrel, and I can go and look through the woods and countryside and see if we can find any trace of her."

Bracken jumped off Mia's knee. "We'll do it tonight."

"We'll find her," said Juniper. "And as soon as we do, we'll let you know."

Mia nodded unhappily, feeling envious of her three friends—their magic didn't seem to come and go like hers.

"You could use your magic to try and find out more about the person doing dark magic," Sita suggested.

Mia shook her head. "It never shows me anything if I ask it to show me that. Just blackness." Bracken had told her it was probably because the person was using dark magic to block herself from being discovered.

She got to her feet. "I think I might go home. I'm feeling a little strange again."

"I'll ask my dad if he'll give you a ride," Violet said.

Mia followed Violet down the stairs. The happiness she had felt when she was doing magic had vanished, and now she just felt angry and disappointed again.

When Mia got back home, she put her school things away, and her eyes fell on the Seeing Stone. She picked it up, wanting to forget the day by looking into the past. She was about to call Bracken's name when she hesitated.

Maybe I won't bother him—he'll be busy trying to find Holly, she told herself. But she knew deep down that it was an excuse, and that really she didn't want him there because he would try and stop her from using the Seeing Stone.

Guilt flared inside her, but she ignored it. "Show me Grandma Anne and Aunt Carol," she whispered to the stone.

A picture appeared in the surface. Grandma Anne and Aunt Carol both looked about fourteen. Aunt Carol had a crystal in her hands and was healing a scratch on Grandma Anne's leg. Grandma Anne hugged her, and then Aunt Carol showed her how she could use a different crystal to cast an illusion—making a rock beside the river appear to turn into a picnic basket. Mia was impressed—Aunt Carol could do so much with her Crystal Magic. Grandma Anne clapped and smiled.

Mia continued to stare into the stone. She lost track of time as she watched image after image of Grandma Anne and Aunt Carol. She only stopped when she felt so tired that she couldn't go on anymore.

She put down the Seeing Stone, feeling as if her energy had been sucked into it. Still, it had been worth it.

Mia placed the stone on her desk and called Bracken. He appeared instantly.

"Mia!" he said. "I've been worried about you. You didn't seem yourself earlier."

"I'm fine." Mia yawned.

Bracken sat back on his haunches. "What have you been doing?" he asked curiously.

"Just stuff." Mia shrugged.

"What stuff?" Bracken asked.

"Nothing important. Stop asking me questions!" Mia's words came out more sharply than she meant them to.

Bracken's ears flattened unhappily. Mia felt bad but couldn't bring herself to say she was sorry. She turned away and started cleaning up her desk. When she looked back, she saw Bracken had jumped onto her bed and was watching her. He looked worried.

The silence stretched between them, awkward and uncomfortable.

"I'm going downstairs to have dinner," Mia muttered, hurrying out of the room.

By the next morning, Mia was still in a bad mood, and it appeared to have spread to the rest of her family. Alex was grouchy, and Cleo was banging things around, trying to find her makeup bag. "Can't you find it for me?" she said to Mia.

"I can't find everything you lose," Mia snapped.

"Girls, please stop bickering!" Mrs. Greene said as Alex started to wail.

Mia grabbed her toast and stomped upstairs, leaving the chaos in the kitchen behind.

When she got to school, she saw Violet waiting on the playground and went over to her. Violet was holding a book on wild animals in Africa. Mia hadn't seen it before.

"Hi," Mia muttered.

"Hi," Violet muttered back.

"What's the book for?" Mia said.

"For Lexi. Her class is doing their projects on endangered animals this week."

Mia felt a stab of jealousy. "Very friendly," she said sarcastically.

Violet frowned. "Are you jealous?" she said. "You are, aren't you? You're jealous that Lexi and I are friends now!"

"Don't be silly!" Mia retorted.

"I'm not the silly one—you are!" Violet shot back.

Just then, Lexi and Sita arrived. Lexi looked grumpy, too, but Sita was smiling as usual. "What's going on?" Sita said, looking at Mia and Violet's angry faces.

"Ask *her*," Violet and Mia muttered at the same time.

Sita looked from one friend to the other.

"Should I use my magic to help you feel better?"

"Oh, yes, your incredibly amazing magic," said Lexi. "You're such a show-off, Sita!"

"I was just trying to help," said Sita, looking upset.

"Sita isn't a show-off!" Mia said angrily.

"You always take her side!" Lexi snapped.

"No, I don't!"

"Why are you all arguing today?" Sita exclaimed.

Their squabble was interrupted by the bell

ringing. The girls picked up their bags and stomped away without saying anything more.

Mia felt like she had a black cloud hanging over her all day. Lexi and Violet seemed to feel the same, and no one suggested meeting up after school. Mia went right home and shut herself in her room. She wanted to use the Seeing Stone to see Grandma Anne again, even though she knew Bracken wouldn't like it. She thought about not calling him, but she didn't want to have to lie to him like she had the night before. Reluctantly, she called his name.

He appeared beside her. "How was school?" he asked.

Mia shrugged. "Not great." She felt suddenly upset with him. Why did he have to make her feel guilty about using the Seeing Stone? She picked it up from her desk. "I'm going to use this to see Grandma Anne."

"Mia, don't," Bracken pleaded.

"But it's better than the mirror," Mia argued. "I don't know why you're so funny about me using it." She stared into it and tried to ignore him. "Show me Grandma Anne when she was younger."

She was soon engrossed in watching Aunt Carol and Grandma Anne doing magic together. When she finally finished, she turned around to find that Bracken had curled into a small ball on her bed. Mia longed to go and cuddle him, but some part of herself stopped her.

It's not like using the Seeing Stone is really bad, she thought irritably. She got changed out of her school clothes without saying a word to Bracken, and then went downstairs. When she came back after dinner, he was gone, and she didn't call his name until bedtime. Then he just curled up quietly by her feet instead of in her arms like he usually did. She turned out the light.

8
A Different Past

When Mia woke up the next morning, she found that Bracken was gone. She glanced at her bedside clock and realized it was much later than usual. Where was he? He usually woke her on school mornings with licks and cuddles.

"Bracken!" she called.

He appeared in her room, beside her bed.

"Where have you been?" she asked, getting up. "You didn't wake me up, and now I'm late for school." She looked at him.

"I… I was out looking for Holly," he said.

Mia felt guilty as she realized she'd forgotten all about the lost dog. "Oh, is that why your paws are muddy?" she said, noticing Bracken's paws were flecked with soil. "Did you find her?" she asked as she started to pull on her school clothes.

"No, there's no trace of her in the woods."

"I hope she's okay," Mia said anxiously. "Maybe I should use the Seeing Stone to try and see her again."

"No, don't!" Bracken said quickly.

Mia frowned. The Seeing Stone wasn't on her desk where she'd left it. She crouched down to check the floor, but just then, her dad knocked on the door and opened it. Bracken vanished just in time.

"Come on, Mia. What are you doing? You're going to be late for school. You need to have some breakfast."

Mia had no choice but to follow her dad

downstairs. *I'll find the Seeing Stone later*, she thought uneasily.

However, when Mia got back from school, she couldn't find the Seeing Stone anywhere. She called Bracken.

"It couldn't have just vanished into thin air," she said. "Have you seen it?"

Bracken scratched his ear with his back paw as he watched her search. "No."

Mia felt a flash of anger. "What am I going to do? I need it!"

"You don't need it," said Bracken, trotting over to her. "You can use Star Magic."

It doesn't work as well, Mia thought, but she didn't say anything to Bracken.

"You can," Bracken insisted, jumping up onto her lap. "Why don't you try now?"

"There's no point," Mia muttered, rubbing his fur. "It won't work."

Bracken cocked his head to one side. "Is that what you think?"

She nodded.

"But Mia, you can't think like that." He looked at her earnestly. "Remember when you first started learning to do magic, and I said it would only happen if you believed it would? If you don't believe the magic will work, it won't."

Mia frowned. She'd forgotten that.

"Seeing magic *is* hard to control," Bracken went on. "But it won't help if you think it's not going to work."

"Maybe I'll try again," Mia said, feeling her bad mood start to fade. She stared into the mirror on the dressing table, petting Bracken as she did. "Show me, Holly," she said, hoping she would get more of an idea of where Holly was this time.

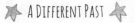

She leaned forward eagerly as an image gradually formed in the mirror, but it just showed Holly surrounded by a lot of snow again. Mia couldn't understand what was going on.

She frowned. Was her magic working? She decided to try something else. "Show me Grandma Anne when she and Aunt Carol were my age," she said.

The surface of the mirror swirled like liquid silver, and Mia's heart gave a leap as an image of Grandma Anne and Aunt Carol appeared. They were both wearing old-fashioned school uniforms. Aunt Carol was glaring at Grandma Anne and speaking angrily. She could hear Aunt Carol saying, "It's not fair! Everyone likes you, Anne. Everyone wants to be your friend. No one wants to be mine!"

"That's not true, Carol," said Grandma Anne. "I'm your friend."

"Yes, but you like everyone!" said Aunt Carol, and then she turned and ran away.

Mia sat back in surprise. She'd never seen Aunt Carol and Grandma Anne arguing before.

"Show me Grandma Anne and Aunt Carol when they start doing magic," she said curiously.

The image changed, and she saw Grandma Anne with her hand on her wolf's back, staring at Aunt Carol, who seemed to be hovering behind a blackberry bush as if she'd been hiding. "You can't tell anyone, Carol," Grandma Anne pleaded. "No one is supposed to know about Star Magic. Promise you won't say a word!"

Mia blinked. Weird. She'd seen this moment in the past before, but it hadn't been like this. When she'd seen it in the Seeing Stone, Grandma Anne had been excitedly telling Aunt Carol that she had a secret to share with her. Now Grandma Anne seemed to be begging Aunt Carol not to say anything—almost as if Grandma Anne hadn't wanted Aunt Carol to know....

"This is odd," Mia whispered to Bracken. "I'm seeing a different past than the one I've seen in the Seeing Stone."

"A different past?" He tilted his head. "But there can't be two pasts."

"I don't know which one is real," said Mia. "Show me more," she said to the mirror.

The image changed, and Mia saw Aunt Carol in the clearing with Grandma Anne. They were older now—teenagers. "I can do magic, too," Aunt Carol was saying to Grandma Anne, showing her a crystal. "It's not just you now. I'm special, too!"

"Yes," Grandma Anne said slowly, "but you must be careful. Magic should only be used for good. Please only do good things with it."

Aunt Carol smiled slyly as she turned the crystal over in her hand. "We'll see."

Mia sat back and let the images fade. "In the

Seeing Stone, I see Grandma Anne and Aunt Carol as really good friends, but when I look with Star Magic, it's not quite like that. Why?"

"I don't know," Bracken said anxiously. "But I think you should believe what the Star Magic is showing you."

Mia rubbed him. "I wish I knew where the Seeing Stone was."

Bracken nuzzled her. "Maybe you should stop doing magic for tonight. We can talk to the other animals tomorrow and see if they have any idea about why the things you're seeing are different."

When Mia went to sleep, she had the first vivid dream she'd had in a long time. Bracken had told her that her dreams might show real things now that her magic was growing stronger. For a while, they had—she'd seen the Fear Shades before they started affecting people—but for the last couple of weeks, her dreams hadn't shown her anything at all. Tonight was different, though.

In her dream, Grandma Anne and Aunt

Carol were in the clearing. They looked about sixteen years old.

Aunt Carol's eyes were shining. "Crystals have energy inside them," she said to Grandma Anne. "All you have to do is figure out how to channel it, and then you can use it for anything you want. You can make an object look like something else! They can heal, hurt, upset—"

"But magic should only be used for good," Grandma Anne interrupted. "You know that."

"But why?" said Aunt Carol. "We could get revenge on people who have made us miserable."

"No!" Grandma Anne exclaimed. "You can't do that."

Aunt Carol smiled. "When I possess the Dark Stone, no one will be able to stop me. Not even you." She laughed.

Mia sat up in bed, her heart pounding. Had her dream been real? It couldn't be. Aunt Carol wouldn't use magic to do bad things. Bracken was still snoozing beside her. Dawn was just breaking, the dark of night turning to a cold gray.

Mia went to her desk to look for the Seeing Stone. How could it have just vanished? Then she looked into the mirror and had an idea. Of course! She could use Star Magic to see where it was.

She opened herself to the magic current. "Show me where the Seeing Stone is."

A picture of her backyard appeared in the mirror.

But how can it be in the yard? she wondered.

"Show me how the Seeing Stone got there," she said curiously.

The image reformed. Ice seemed to run down her spine as she saw a fox trotting toward the flower bed just as dawn was breaking. It was Bracken, and he had the Seeing Stone in his mouth. She watched as he dropped it onto the soil, dug a hole, and nudged it inside.

Bracken had taken the Seeing Stone. He had

lied to her! Unless … unless what she was seeing was false.

"Bracken!" she said, swinging around.

He woke instantly. "What is it?" he said, jumping to his feet.

"Did you take the Seeing Stone?" she demanded. "Did you bury it in the yard?" She was sure he was going to shake his head and tell her that what she had seen wasn't true.

But he looked down at the bed. "Yes," he admitted. "I'm sorry. But I didn't like you using it. There's something strange about it, Mia. I think it's showing you a false past, and I think it's doing something to your Star Magic…."

"How dare you!" Mia hissed. She grabbed her robe and slippers. "I'm going to get it back!"

"Mia!" Bracken protested. "Don't go!"

"You're the one who should go," Mia said. "I don't want you here!"

Bracken whimpered. "You don't mean that."

"I do! Go!"

Mia ran out of her room, down the stairs, and
through the back door. A light frost covered the
grass, and the air stung her cheeks. She ran to
the flower bed that she had seen in the mirror
and spotted a patch of soil that looked like it had
been recently disturbed. Crouching down, she
used her hands to dig into the freezing soil. She
caught a glimmer of pink and pushed the soil
to one side. It was the Seeing Stone! She took it
out with a sigh of relief.

When she came back into the house, her dad was in the kitchen getting Alex a bottle of milk.

"Mia!" he exclaimed. "What on earth are you doing out in the yard at this hour?"

"I'd left something out there," Mia lied.

"Well, you don't go out at six in the morning! And look at the mess you're making on the carpet."

"I'm sorry," Mia said. "I'll clean it up."

"Just take off your slippers and get back upstairs," her dad snapped. "I don't want this to happen again."

Mia kicked off her slippers and ran upstairs. When she got back to her room, it was empty. Bracken was gone.

9
MAKING PLANS

Mia shut the door and walked slowly over to her bed. Her eyes filled with hot, stinging tears. Everything was wrong. Everyone was angry and arguing, and Bracken…. She thought back to how she had told him to go, and a sudden fear gripped her. He wouldn't have gone back to the Star World, would he? He *was* still her Star Animal, right?

She sat on the bed and put her face in her hands.

"Bracken," she whispered.

She held her breath. Nothing happened. Her heart felt like it was going to break into pieces.

"Bracken!" she whispered frantically.

She almost fainted with relief when a shimmer of starlight slowly appeared, a curling plume of light getting stronger until it turned into the shape of a fox.

Bracken stood across the room from her, his ears lowered sadly and his tail between his legs.

"Bracken!" Mia gasped, holding out her arms.

He crept slowly over to her, wagging the tip of his bushy tail, and she gathered him into her arms.

"I thought you'd gone back to the Star World," she said, a tear spilling down her cheek. "I thought I wasn't ever going to see you again."

He licked the tear away. "You're my Star Friend, Mia. That means I'll be with you for your whole life. If you call me, I'll always come."

"I'm sorry." Mia hugged him as tightly as she could. As he snuggled in her arms, she felt the anger that had been filling her mind drain away.

"I'm sorry I took the Seeing Stone, and I'm sorry I lied to you," he told her. "I just don't like that stone. I think there's something strange about it."

"I won't use it again," said Mia. "And I… I'm sorry I snapped at you the other day. I've just felt so mixed up and confused. It's like there's a cloud in my head making me feel angry all the time at the moment." She frowned. "Though it's not there now."

Bracken looked thoughtful. "I wonder if…." He broke off. "Stay there. Let's try something." He wriggled out of her arms and trotted across her bedroom. "How do you feel now?"

Irritation started to flicker through Mia. "Worse again."

Bracken bounded back and jumped into her arms. "And now?" he said, nuzzling her neck.

The feelings faded.

"Better," said Mia. She frowned at him. "So, when I'm hugging you, I feel normal. Why?"

"The bad feelings must be caused by some sort of dark magic," Bracken said, his indigo eyes serious. "That's why they go away when you're hugging me."

"Do you think there's a Shade in the house?" said Mia, looking around her room. "Everyone in my family has been in a bad mood. Lexi and Violet, too. Do you think there are a lot of Shades?"

"Maybe," said Bracken. "I think we need to speak to the others."

"I'll ask them to meet me before school," said Mia. She jumped up to get her phone. As soon as she was no longer holding Bracken, she could feel the bad mood starting to take over again, but she tried to fight the feelings away. *I'm not upset*, she told herself firmly. *I'm not angry*. She sent a group message to the others.

Must talk to you at school. It's important. Get there early. Mxx

A few seconds later, her phone pinged. It was a message from Lexi.

I can't. Gotta go to dentist Lx

Mia wanted to talk to everyone together. She texted back:

Okay. Let's meet at recess and talk then.

Her phone pinged once more. It was Violet.

What's going on? Vx

Tell u later. But for now cuddle ur animals a lot.

WHAT?!!

Sita joined in.

I don't understand. Sxxx

Talk at schl. Try not to get angry. Mxx

And then, ignoring the flurry of question marks and confused emojis that started showing up on her phone from her friends, she gathered Bracken into her arms and hugged him tightly.

✦ ✦ ✦

"So, you're saying you think Shades have been making us argue?" Violet said in a low voice as they sat on the wall at recess. They were all wrapped up in coats and scarves and hats against the cold.

Mia nodded. "We don't normally feel like this, do we? We don't usually fall out like we did yesterday. My family has been in bad moods, too."

"And mine," said Lexi. "Mom's been shouting all the time."

Violet nodded. "Mine, too."

"Mine haven't," said Sita, looking puzzled.
"And I haven't felt angry. I have felt unhappy,
but that's just because everyone's been
arguing."

Mia looked at Lexi and Violet. "But you've
felt like me? Like there's something making
you feel angry with everyone."

They both nodded.

"I shouted at Sorrel yesterday," Violet
admitted.

"And I got upset with Juniper," said Lexi.

"I told Bracken to go away," said Mia.

"It's got to be because of Shades," Sita said.
"Maybe they're just affecting me differently."

Lexi rolled her eyes. "Oh, because you're
so special!" Her hand flew to her mouth. "I'm
sorry!" she gasped. "I didn't mean that, Sita! I
don't know why I said it. I feel all twisted up
inside with horrible feelings. Mia's right. It's *got*
to be because of Shades."

"But where are they? What are they trapped in this time?" said Violet. "Why haven't Sorrel or Willow smelled them? They're both really good at sniffing out Shades."

"I don't know," said Mia. "Should we meet up after school and try to figure it out?"

"I can't. I'm going over to my grandma's," Sita said.

"And I have piano until six," said Lexi.

"I could ask Sorrel to check my house really well," said Violet. "And then later I'll shadow-travel to Mia and Lexi's and bring us all to yours, Sita. Can you make sure no one is in your clubhouse? We could meet there."

Sita nodded.

"Okay, Mia and Lexi, be ready in your bedrooms at six-thirty. Agreed?" said Violet.

Mia felt a rush of irritation that Violet was taking charge, but she pushed it firmly away. "Okay. And in the meantime, let's try really hard not to argue."

They all nodded. "Agreed."

Mia found it hard to concentrate at school that day. She realized she hadn't told the others about the different pasts she had seen when she was using the Seeing Stone and the Star Magic, but right now, it felt more important to stop the Shades that were making them argue.

When she got home, she shut herself away in her bedroom with Bracken and lay on her bed cuddling him. A little later, she got a text from Sita.

How r u? Sxxx

OK. Did u see ur grandma?

Yes. She wasn't in a v good mood, either.
Maybe there are Shades EVERYWHERE!

Mia bit her lip.

Want to talk? Mxx

After a few seconds, her phone started to
ring with a video call from Sita.

Mia answered it, and Sita's face appeared on
her screen. She looked upset.

"What if I'm right? What if there are Shades
everywhere, and they're affecting everyone?"
she said.

"We'll get rid of them," Mia told her. "We're
Star Friends. You'll be able to command them
like you did with the stretchy men."

"If it works," said Sita. "I haven't tried it
since…. Mia, what if it doesn't?"

"It will," Mia told her. "But first we have to
find the Shades. Did Willow notice any trace at
your house?"

"Nothing," said Sita. "But maybe Sorrel has found something at Violet's."

"I hope so," said Mia.

When it got close to six-thirty, they hung up, and Mia waited for Violet to appear. Even though she was expecting it, she still jumped when Violet and Lexi stepped out of the shadows beside her closet.

"Let's get to Sita's," Violet said, holding out her hand.

Mia stepped into the shadows with Violet and Lexi and felt the strange sensation of the world spinning away around her. Then her feet touched solid ground, and she realized that she was standing in Sita's clubhouse. It was a garden shed that Sita and her sisters had put a rug and some beanbags in.

Sita had turned on a small table light, casting shadows against the shed walls. "We can't be long," she said anxiously. "Our parents might start wondering where we are."

"Did Sorrel find anything?" Mia asked Violet.

"No, nothing," Violet said. "She went through my whole house, and she didn't smell a Shade anywhere."

"But there have to be Shades there!" said Mia.

"Maybe magic can disguise the smell," said Lexi.

"I asked Sorrel that," Violet said. "She said nothing can hide the smell of Shades."

"It doesn't make sense," said Mia. "The bad

moods have to be caused by Shades, because otherwise, they wouldn't fade like they do when we're cuddling our animals."

Sita glanced out the window anxiously. "I'm going to have to go inside in a minute."

"Let's meet up tomorrow morning," said Mia. "Is everyone free?"

They found out they were all free except for Lexi, who had gymnastics. "I can meet you right after," she said.

"Why don't we meet at my house at twelve," said Violet. "We can go to the clearing in the woods. Maybe we'll think better when we're there because Sorrel says the current of magic is so strong."

"Then it's the Christmas fair in the afternoon," said Mia.

Sita shivered. "It's creepy to think that the person doing dark magic might actually be there. We might speak to her without realizing it."

"We've got to make a list of everyone we see

there who matches the description," said Lexi. "The sooner we find out who it is, the better!"

Violet shadow-traveled them all home. After Mia had whispered good-bye and her friends had disappeared, she sat down at her desk feeling very confused. If there were Shades affecting them all, why couldn't Sorrel and Willow find any trace of them?

I don't get it, she thought, resting her chin on her hands and staring into the mirror. *I don't understand.*

10
A TROUBLING VISIT

Mia's dreams that night showed her a gloomy underground room with stone walls. She was trapped, unable to move and overwhelmed by the feeling that she had lost something precious. A woman in a hooded cloak stalked up to her with a dark crystal in her hand. Mia could not see her face.

"When I touch you with this, you will lose everything," hissed the woman. She lifted it toward Mia.

"No!" Mia screamed.

She woke with a start to find Bracken licking her face. "You were having a bad dream, Mia. You were calling out in your sleep."

Mia pulled Bracken into a hug, burying her face in his soft fur, and told him what she'd seen.

"What did the woman look like?" Bracken asked. "Was it anyone you recognized?"

"I couldn't see her face." Mia shuddered as she remembered the fear she'd felt.

Bracken cuddled her closer. "We have to figure out what's going on. Maybe when you go to the fair this afternoon, you'll find some clues about who the lady is who's doing all this."

"I hope so," said Mia.

She lay in bed and petted Bracken until it was time to get up.

She was just getting dressed when her phone pinged.

It was a message from Sita.

What r u doing this morning? Sxx

Nothing. What about u?

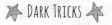

Nothing much either. I didn't sleep v well. Think I might go and see Aunt Carol and have a talk with her about my power.

Good plan. Come here afterward if u want.

OK! Sxx

Mia put her phone into her pocket and kissed Bracken. "I'm going to get some breakfast. Sita's coming over later. Maybe we can do some magic with her and Willow."

She went downstairs. Her mom was banging breakfast bowls on the table. "Are you okay?" Mia asked tentatively.

"No, not really. I have so much to do," her mom said. "I need to help set up for the fair this morning, but I also have to show someone Grandma Anne's house. And I said I would stop by and help Aunt Carol take some boxes of decorations to the hall."

"I can do that," said Mia. Then she could meet Sita there, and they could both talk to Aunt Carol. Maybe Aunt Carol would be able to help her figure out why she was seeing two different versions of the past.

"Well, I was going to drive the boxes of decorations to the hall," her mom said, "but I'm sure they're light enough for you to carry. That would really help." She smiled. "Thanks, sweetie."

"No problem. I'll go after breakfast," Mia said, putting some bread in the toaster.

After breakfast, Mia ran upstairs to tell Bracken what she was doing. "I'll be back as soon as I can," she said.

"All right." He licked her nose as she hugged him. "I'll see you later."

He jumped onto the bed and curled up into a ball, his nose tucked into his bushy tail.

Mia smiled. "I love you," she whispered, giving him a kiss. She picked up the Seeing Stone so she could ask Aunt Carol about it and texted Sita as she headed out.

Are u at AC's yet? I'll c u there. Mxx

Mia rode her bike quickly to keep warm. By the time she reached Aunt Carol's house, her cheeks were pink, and she was slightly breathless.

"Good morning," said Aunt Carol, opening the door when she knocked. "What are you doing here, Mia?"

"I've come to help you take the decorations to the hall—Mom's really busy with other things," said Mia.

"That's very kind of you," said Aunt Carol.

"Is Sita here?" Mia asked.

Aunt Carol looked surprised. "Sita? No. Why? Was she planning on visiting me?"

Mia nodded. "She's going to drop by this morning. She wants to talk to you about magic," she said as Aunt Carol ushered her inside.

"Well, why don't I get you a hot chocolate while we're waiting for her?" said Aunt Carol. "You go on into the living room, and I'll put the kettle on."

As Aunt Carol hurried to the kitchen, Mia took off her coat and hung it in the hall, making a mental note that Aunt Carol seemed as cheerful as usual. *No Shades affecting her,* she thought as she went into the living room.

The boxes of knitted decorations sat on the coffee table. Mia picked one up, and its black crystal eyes sparkled in the light. Although the decoration looked cute, the crystal reminded Mia of the dark crystal she had seen in her dream. She shivered and put down the decoration.

The large snow globe she had seen the last time she was here was standing on the mantel. She went over to it and saw that it now had a little model of a brown and white dog inside, curled up, fast asleep. How had Aunt Carol put that in there?

Magic? wondered Mia.

Then the dog yawned and sat up.

Mia squeaked in shock. The dog was moving! It shook itself and sniffed around in the snow. Mia stared. What amazing magic was making the model dog seem alive?

She skirted around it to examine the globe from a different angle. The little brown and white dog looked strangely familiar, Mia decided. It looked just like Holly, the Patels' missing dog! As she stepped to the side to get a closer look, she stepped on something soft and glanced down to see a blue and white scarf with a polka-dot pattern. Mia froze. It was Sita's favorite scarf.

But Aunt Carol had just told her that Sita hadn't stopped by.

Her fingers tightened on the soft fabric, unease quickening through her as she looked from the scarf to the snow globe. What was going on?

Then she heard a faint banging sound coming from the hallway. Picking up the snow globe, she hurried to the living room doorway.

Thump, thump, thump.

The noise was coming from the door under the stairs. Mia knew that it led to Aunt Carol's cellar. Her heart skipped a beat as she heard a faint voice. "Let me out! Please, let me out!"

"Sita?" Mia gasped in shock.

"Mia! Get me out of here!" Sita exclaimed.

Mia put the snow globe on the floor and started to pull the stiff metal bolts on the door.

"What are you doing in there?" she whispered as she tried to wriggle the top bolt back.

"Aunt Carol locked me in," said Sita, her voice faint through the door. "Mia, we've got to get out of here. She's not good like we thought."

Mia felt like all the breath had left her body. "What?"

"She's trapped Holly in the snow globe! She's evil!" Sita said.

There was a laugh behind her. Mia spun around and saw Aunt Carol standing in the kitchen doorway, watching her with an amused look in her eyes.

11
TRAPPED!

Aunt Carol's smile widened as Mia stared at her.

"Mia!" Sita banged on the door, breaking Mia out of her shock. "What's happening?"

Throwing herself at the door again, Mia scrambled to pull back the bolts.

"Bracken!" she gasped. "Please come! I need you!"

He appeared in a shimmer of starlight just as Aunt Carol pulled a dark crystal from her pocket and held it out toward the door,

muttering a harsh-sounding word that Mia had
never heard before. The metal bolts instantly
turned red-hot.

Mia yelped and pulled her hands away, her
fingers stinging.

"Let Sita out!" shouted Mia as Bracken
bounded at Aunt Carol, his teeth bared, and
stopped in front of her, growling angrily. "Why
have you locked her up?"

Aunt Carol grabbed the snow globe from
the floor where Mia had left it.

"Because I am going to stop you Star
Friends from getting in my way," Aunt Carol
said. She held the snow globe in one hand
and a large, glittering dark crystal in the
other.

A shiver ran down Mia's spine as she
recognized the crystal from her dream.

Bracken sprang forward, and for a moment,
Mia thought he was going to be able to snatch
it—but then Aunt Carol swung the snow

globe at him. The instant it touched his fur, he vanished.

Mia stared at the empty space where he had been. "Bracken!" Her voice rose. "What have you done with him?"

Aunt Carol held up the snow globe with a triumphant smile. Inside the globe, next to the little dog, there was now a small russet fox. "He's in here. And unless you do what I say, you won't ever see him again."

"Bracken!" Mia whispered, horrified.

Bracken started to bark furiously—Mia could see his mouth opening and closing, but she couldn't hear him. Aunt Carol touched the Dark Stone to the bolts of the cellar door, and they slid back on their own, opening the door.

There was a flash of brown, and Willow came charging out, heading straight for Aunt Carol.

"Willow! Be careful!" cried Sita.

Moving more swiftly than Mia would have
thought possible, Aunt Carol swept the globe
toward Willow, and as it touched her back, the
deer vanished.

"Two Star Animals are mine, just two to
go!" crowed Aunt Carol, holding up the globe.
Inside, Willow was standing next to Bracken,
shaking her head and looking very surprised.

"Into the cellar with your friend!" Aunt
Carol commanded, looking at Mia.

"No." Mia shook her head. "I'm not going
in there."

"If you don't, I will smash the globe. And what will happen to your precious animals then?" Aunt Carol's eyes met Mia's. "They'll be gone forever!" She held the globe high above the floor.

"Stop it!" Sita cried, but Aunt Carol ignored her.

Mia hesitated. What should she do? Aunt Carol's hand started to swing the globe downward.

"No! Wait!" Mia gasped. "I'll go in the cellar."

She joined Sita, and with a harsh laugh, Aunt Carol swung the door shut, plunging them into darkness. As they heard the bolts being pushed across, Sita grabbed Mia's hands. "What are we going to do?"

"I… I don't know." Mia was struggling to take everything in. Bracken was gone, and so was Willow…. She and Sita were trapped…. And Aunt Carol had been the person using dark magic!

Mia peered through the gloom. They were at the top of a staircase that led down into the cellar. "Isn't there a light in here?"

"I haven't been able to find one," said Sita.

Mia drew on her magic. It tingled through her and her eyesight sharpened, letting her see through the gloom.

"There!" she said, spotting an old-fashioned metal light switch high up on the wall. Standing on tiptoe, she pressed it, and a bulb in the ceiling lit up. It cast a weak light. At the bottom of the wooden stairs, the shadows in the cellar seemed to make everything look menacing. Still, it was better to have some light than none at all.

"What's she going to do to Bracken and Willow?" said Sita.

"I don't know." Mia felt panic rising inside her, but she forced it down. Panicking wouldn't help them—or their animals. "We have to get them out of that globe." She frowned. "How did you end up trapped here?"

Sita shivered. "When I came over to talk to Aunt Carol, she said she would make me some hot chocolate. As I was drinking it, I noticed the snow globe. Did you see it? Holly's inside!"

"I know! I saw!" Mia said. "Then I noticed your scarf on the floor."

"I must have dropped it when I saw Holly," Sita went on. "I think Aunt Carol put something in the hot chocolate. All I can remember is jumping up to leave but then feeling really dizzy. I must have passed out because when I woke up, I was in here. I called Willow and started banging on the door, and then I heard you on the other side. Now you're in here, too!" Her eyes filled with tears.

Mia hugged her. "Aunt Carol can't keep us in here forever," she said. "When she comes back, you'll have to use your commanding magic and make her let us out."

"It doesn't work," said Sita. "I tried when she was about to smash the globe, but it didn't make any difference."

Mia's heart sank. "You were trying to use your magic then?"

Sita nodded. "I can't do it. I told you. It was just a fluke with the stretchy men." She wiped away her tears with the back of her hand. "I'm not that powerful."

"Don't worry," Mia said. "I'll come up with another way to get us out." She thought back over the last few months. So, Aunt Carol had been the person doing evil all along. She must have attached the stretchy men to the boxes of sparklers herself. Mia remembered what the sales assistant at the garden center had said to

Violet and Lexi—an older lady with gray hair and blue eyes had bought the Wish Gnome. That must have been Aunt Carol, too. And then there was the very first Shade they had faced— the one who had been trapped inside the old compact mirror talking to Cleo. A picture flashed into Mia's mind of Aunt Carol helping her mom clean out Grandma Anne's house....

"Look what I just found in a drawer," she'd said, turning around to Mia with the compact mirror in her hand.

Maybe she took it with her and gave it to me on purpose, Mia realized. *She wanted* me *to be affected by the Shade—only I gave the compact to Cleo. Aunt Carol found the compact just after I had told her I had seen a fox with indigo eyes. She must have realized I was going to be a Star Friend.*

She felt sick. She had trusted Aunt Carol. She had told her about Bracken and let her see the Star Animals. She had asked her for advice and taken it. When she had tried to do what Aunt Carol said, her magic had stopped working, too. Why hadn't she realized?

Because I thought Aunt Carol was Grandma Anne's friend!

Mia remembered the two different pasts she had seen—one using Star Magic and one using the Seeing Stone. She pulled the pink Seeing Stone out of her pocket and it glittered in the dim light. No wonder Bracken hadn't liked it. It had been showing her lies about the past. She looked at the golden glow coming from it and groaned inwardly. She should have realized. Whenever something was under an illusion spell, she saw a glow around it. "I don't believe you look like you do," she whispered.

The glow faded, and the stone turned an ugly gray with a red eye-shape in the center.

"What's that stone?" Sita said curiously.

"Aunt Carol gave it to me," Mia said. "She told me it would help me see into the past, but it hasn't been showing me the real past.

It's been showing me a past she wanted me to see. Aunt Carol wanted me to think that she and Grandma Anne were really good friends. I guess she did it so that I would trust her."

"But they *were* friends, weren't they?" Sita said, looking confused. "Didn't your grandma visit her a lot?"

Mia nodded. She didn't understand that part. Why *had* Grandma Anne visited Aunt Carol so often if Aunt Carol was evil?

She threw the Seeing Stone away from her, down the stairs into the shadows, and heard it clatter onto the stone floor.

Just then, there was the sound of the bolts pulling back. The girls jumped to their feet as the door opened and Aunt Carol stood there, smiling at them, the snow globe in one hand, the Dark Stone in the other.

12
A Desperate Situation

"Let us go!" Sita said. She took a breath, and Mia could tell she was trying to use her commanding magic. Her voice shook. "You must let us out of here."

Aunt Carol laughed. "Oh, no. You're not going anywhere."

She held up the glittering Dark Stone, and Mia cried out as a stream of energy seemed to thump into her stomach. Arms windmilling, she fell backward, and she and Sita tumbled down the stairs in a tangle of arms and legs.

They landed in a heap in the cellar. Aunt
Carol chuckled and followed them down to
the bottom.

For a moment, Mia was winded and
struggled to breathe. She rolled onto her knees,
drawing in gasps of air, and saw that Sita was
doing the same.

Mia was aware of Aunt Carol moving swiftly
around them. But it was only as she got her
breath back that she realized Aunt Carol had
drawn a circle around them using the stone,
leaving a glowing red line on the floor. Aunt

Carol straightened up and muttered a word. Instantly, an assortment of candles standing on ledges around the stone cellar lit up. They cast a flickering glow, letting Mia see that they were in a large underground room with a table at one end covered in rocks and crystals.

"What are you doing?" Mia demanded, standing up and helping Sita to her feet.

"I'm using the Dark Stone to make sure you can't escape," said Aunt Carol coldly. "I will keep you here until your friends arrive. When I have their Star Animals, too, I will use the Dark Stone to take away all your memories of magic. I will make you forget you ever knew about Star Animals and the Star World. When you stop believing in magic, you will no longer stand in my way."

"We'll never stop believing in magic!" exclaimed Mia.

Aunt Carol's eyes glittered. "You will not be able to resist the Dark Stone. It is one of the most powerful crystals in the world. You're going to have to say good-bye to your animals."

She held out the snow globe. Bracken put up his paws on the glass, looking desperately at Mia. She lunged forward, but flames leaped up from the glowing line on the floor, licking at her outstretched arms. Mia sprang back.

"Why are you doing this?" shouted Sita.

"Why?" Aunt Carol raised her eyebrows. "So that I can be the most powerful. More powerful than any Star Friend will ever be."

"I thought you and Grandma Anne were friends!" Mia said furiously, her eyes stinging with tears. "I thought you did good magic!"

Aunt Carol snorted. "That's what she would have liked. But then I found the Dark Stone, and I knew that when I learned to use it, I would be able to do anything I wanted." Her voice grew bitter. "But before I could learn to use its powers properly, Anne managed to take it from me and use her commanding magic to stop me from taking it back. Every time she visited me, she reinforced the command—and without the Dark Stone, I was powerless to fight back."

"So that's why she visited you so often," Mia said slowly.

Aunt Carol gave a nod. "People thought we were friends, but really, she was just trying to get me to lead a normal life. A dull life without magic and power while she—" her eyes filled with jealousy—"could continue doing her magic. She had her Star Animal. I had nothing!"

"She stopped you because you were going

to use magic for bad things," said Mia. "You wanted to hurt people—just like you're doing now." She looked at the stone. "But how did you get the stone back?"

"Oh, I was so helpful when your grandma died, wasn't I?" Aunt Carol said with a sly smile. "I offered to clean through all her things, and I found it. It was as if it was waiting for me." Her fingers clenched around it. "Now it's mine, and I am going to use it to hurt all the people Anne wanted to protect."

"What do you mean?" said Sita.

"Those knitted decorations upstairs are so sweet, aren't they?" said Aunt Carol. "I'm sure they'll sell out at the fair today. Once they're in houses all around town, they'll start to affect people, little by little."

"The decorations?" Mia said. "But they don't have Shades in them. Sorrel checked."

"Oh, my dear, you have so much to learn. It's not only Shades that can cause trouble," said

Aunt Carol. "Herbs, potions, crystals, spells—
they can all be used to release negative energy
that will hurt and harm. Like that Seeing Stone
I glamoured and gave to you. It showed you
a false past, and it has also been sending out
negative energy to block your magic and stop
it from working."

Mia stared at her. Now that she thought
about it, she realized it was true. Aunt Carol
laughed at her stunned expression.

"You really have been so easy to deceive.
Those crystals I carefully sewed into the eyes
of the decorations will send out their negative
energy. People will start to be affected, and
unhappiness will come. But no one will ever
suspect the innocent little decorations. No one
will be having a good Christmas in Westport
this year." She smiled in delight.

"We'll stop you!" Mia exclaimed.

"How?" said Aunt Carol, raising her
eyebrows. "You're trapped here. Soon your

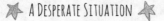

friends will be here with you, too, and then
I will take all your memories of magic away.
If you don't believe, you can't make magic
happen."

"But how will you get the others to come
here?" said Sita.

"By using a little illusion combined with
modern technology." Her voice hardened.
"Star Friends always think they're so special.
But Crystal Magic is better. You each only
have a few powers—I can do many things!"
She walked to the table and put down the
snow globe. Then she held up the Dark Stone
and whispered Mia's name. The air seemed to
shiver, and Aunt Carol changed to look just like
Mia. "What do you think?"

"You won't fool Lexi and Violet!" Mia
declared.

"You don't sound like Mia," said Sita.

Aunt Carol held the stone to her throat and
muttered another word.

"I'll be back very soon," she said in Mia's voice and then, picking up the snow globe, she laughed and headed up the stairs.

13
WHAT NOW?

"What are we going to do?" Mia said desperately as they heard the cellar door shut.

"I don't know," said Sita. "But let me heal the burn on your arm first." She took Mia's arm, and Mia felt as if a cooling breeze was sweeping over her skin, taking away the heat and pain. She watched the blisters disappear and the pinkness fade.

"Thank you," she said gratefully.

"At least I can still do that type of magic," said Sita with relief.

"I bet you can do your commanding magic, too," said Mia. Sita shook her head, but Aunt Carol's words were echoing in Mia's head: *If you don't believe, you can't make magic happen.* It reminded her of what Bracken had said. "When you try to do it, do you believe it will work?"

Sita hesitated. "Um … not really, I guess. It's not how I feel with healing magic. I know that will work."

"You need to believe your commanding magic will work, too," said Mia. "When the Seeing Stone was affecting me, I stopped thinking that my Star Magic would show me the past. Even when I wasn't near the Seeing Stone, it didn't work. But once I believed it would, it did." Mia looked around for some way to escape. Right now, persuading Sita her magic would work wasn't the priority. "We need to get to Violet and Lexi somehow and warn them."

Sita gasped. "My phone! We could use it to text them!" She pulled it out of her pocket and tried to turn it on, but then her face fell. "It's not working. The battery must be dead."

"Or the magic in here is stopping it somehow," said Mia.

"Where's yours?" said Sita.

"In my coat in the hallway," said Mia. "We've got to think of a plan. I wonder how much time we have. If Aunt Carol is going to persuade Lexi and Violet to come here, it'll take her a little while. I can use my magic to see where they are." She took the mirror out of her pocket and tried to relax. "Lexi," she whispered.

An image of Lexi appeared. She was just going into Violet's house. "They're at Violet's," Mia said to Sita. She watched Violet and Lexi run upstairs and go into Violet's bedroom.

"The others will be here soon," she heard Violet say. "I wonder if we'll find out anything about the person doing dark magic at the fair this afternoon."

Suddenly, Violet's phone rang, and she picked it up from her desk. "Mia's calling me."

Mia frowned. Aunt Carol must have taken her phone! "Don't answer it!" she pleaded, even though she knew they couldn't hear her.

"What's happening?" demanded Sita.

Mia shook her head—she needed to see what was happening. Violet was answering the call, and a picture of Mia popped up on her screen. "Hi, it's me."

It was really odd for Mia to hear her own voice.

"Where are you?" Violet asked, holding up the phone so Lexi could join in with the call.

"At Aunt Carol's. I need you both to come here quickly."

"Why?" said Lexi.

"I've found something very important in the cellar. Come now."

"Okay," said Violet. "But what is it?"

"I'll tell you when you get here."

The phone went blank.

Mia's face paled, and she told Sita what had just happened.

"We've got to think of some way to stop them," said Sita.

There was a crash and a clatter beside the table, and Violet and Lexi appeared in the shadows with Sorrel and Juniper.

Mia's heart plummeted. It was too late.

Sorrel took one sniff of the air, and her tail fluffed up in alarm.

"What's going on?" Violet demanded, hurrying toward Mia and Sita.

Sorrel yowled and leaped in front of Violet, knocking her over. Violet sprawled on the stone floor. "What did you do that for?" she gasped.

"Dark magic!" Sorrel hissed, her indigo eyes flashing as she looked at the circle on the floor. She spun around, taking in everything in the room. "This place reeks of it!"

"Sorrel's right," Mia said. "Whatever you do, don't try and cross over the circle drawn on the floor. Flames jump up at you. You'll get burned."

Violet scrambled to her feet, and Lexi joined her. Juniper was next to her, looking around anxiously.

"What's going on?" Lexi demanded again.

Mia and Sita told them about Aunt Carol. They both looked stunned.

"I knew it!" spat Sorrel. "When we were in her yard last time, I smelled Shades."

"We thought it was because of Mrs. Crooks," said Mia, "but it must have been because of Aunt Carol. She has a stone that's really powerful. Grandma Anne took it from her a long time ago and then visited her every day to keep commanding her not to use dark magic. But when Grandma Anne died, Aunt Carol got the stone back."

"I just can't believe it," said Lexi, shaking her head.

"It's true," said Sita. She told them about the illusion Aunt Carol had cast to make herself look and sound like Mia. "She's probably waiting for you at the front door right now."

"Why did you come to the cellar?" said Mia.

"Well, you said you'd found something important here—I wanted to find out what it was," said Violet.

"Violet's so brave," said Sorrel, purring approvingly and weaving between Violet's legs.

"I tried to stop her," said Lexi. "Though I'm

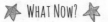

kind of glad she didn't listen to me now. At least we didn't walk right into a trap."

"Where are Bracken and Willow?" said Juniper looking around.

Mia's heart twisted. "They're stuck inside a snow globe and Holly, the Patels' dog, is with them!" she explained. "It must be why I kept seeing Holly in snow. Aunt Carol told me she was going to test the globe. I think she tried out the magic on Holly—maybe because Mrs. Patel was one of Grandma Anne's friends and she wanted to hurt her, just like she's been trying to hurt me and my family. Now Bracken and Willow are trapped inside it, too."

Juniper chattered unhappily, and Sorrel bristled. "This is very bad news," she said. "If the elderly woman has them in her power, you'll have to do as she says."

"We've got to be able to stop her somehow," said Violet desperately.

At that moment, the cellar door opened.

"Hide!" Mia mouthed quickly.

Lexi hid behind the table while Violet ran to the wall and cast a glamour. She immediately seemed to merge with the wall. Juniper and Sorrel disappeared.

"Your friends will be here very soon," said Aunt Carol, coming down the stairs with the snow globe. She looked her usual self again. "But I don't think we need to wait for them to begin. It's time to start taking away your memories of magic." She touched the Dark Stone to the floor, and the circle around Mia and Sita vanished. "Who is going to be first?" she said with an evil smile.

A Shade stepped out from the shadows by the wall. It was tall and thin, with spiny fingers and sharp teeth. "How about me?" it hissed, flexing its fingers.

14
SHOWDOWN

Aunt Carol exclaimed in shock. Mia froze, but then she noticed the Shade had a glowing golden outline and realized it was Violet using her magic to cast an illusion.

"What are you doing here? Who conjured you from the shadows?" Aunt Carol backed away and stumbled on the Seeing Stone that Mia had thrown into the cellar earlier. Losing her balance, she fell to the ground.

There was a sudden blur of movement—it was Lexi darting out from behind the table.

She grabbed the snow globe from Aunt Carol's hands before the elderly lady realized what was happening.

"No!" shrieked Aunt Carol, scrambling after her on her hands and knees. But Lexi was already safely on the other side of the room, cradling the snow globe in her hands.

The Shade became Violet once more. "Smash the globe, Lexi!"

"If you do, the animals will disappear forever!" hissed Aunt Carol.

Violet hesitated, but then she shook her head. "No, I don't believe you. When we smashed the mirror, it *released* the Mirror Shade."

"Yes, and when the garden gnome smashed, it set the Wish Shade inside it free," said Lexi.

"You're right!" urged Juniper, leaping onto the table with the crystals. "Do it, Lexi!"

Aunt Carol held up the Dark Stone and opened her mouth.

Mia's heart leaped into her throat. She was sure Aunt Carol was going to use some sort of horrible power on Lexi. She couldn't let that happen. Throwing herself at Aunt Carol, she grabbed the stone and wrestled it out of her fingers. "Got it!" she gasped in triumph.

Aunt Carol's eyes glittered. "And so you have!" she spat. She pointed at Mia from the floor and screamed out a string of harsh-sounding words that Mia couldn't understand.

Mia felt the world spin, and then it seemed as though her head was getting lighter and lighter. Her thoughts grew fuzzy and confused, and all she could hear were the strange-sounding words. She sank down to her knees, still holding the Dark Stone in her hands.

"What's happening?" Mia heard Violet cry. "What's she doing to Mia?"

"Stop it!" Sita shouted, pointing at Aunt Carol. Her voice was suddenly strong and clear. "I command you to be silent!"

Aunt Carol's mouth opened and closed, but no sound came out. With a yowl, Sorrel pounced on the elderly lady's chest, and Lexi threw the globe onto the floor. There was a huge smash, and it exploded into a million pieces.

The next instant, Bracken and Willow were in the room with the girls. Bracken raced over to Mia and started licking her face. Willow charged to Sita's side and rubbed her head against her. Holly, the spaniel, scurried under the table fearfully.

Mia started to pet the fox, but then she stopped. Why was she petting a fox? He seemed very tame.

She looked around. Why was she in a cellar with her friends? And why were there so many animals? And why was that wildcat sitting on poor Aunt Carol's chest and hissing furiously at her? "What's happening?" she said in confusion.

"Mia!" the fox said, nuzzling her cheek. "Are you all right?"

Mia blinked. She could have sworn she'd just heard him say her name. But that couldn't be right. Animals couldn't talk. She stood up and backed away from the fox. "What … what's going on?" she said faintly. She realized she was holding a dark sparkling stone in her hand and dropped it.

The red squirrel raced over and grabbed it in his paws.

"Stay where you are, Aunt Carol. I command you to freeze!" Sita said to Aunt Carol as she lunged at the squirrel.

Aunt Carol stopped with a jerk.

"What's happening?" Violet said. "Why is Mia being weird?"

"I didn't silence Aunt Carol in time," said Sita. "I think she said the spell—and now Mia has forgotten everything about magic."

"Magic?" Mia echoed in confusion. "What

are you talking about? Magic isn't real."

Seeing her friends exchange horrified looks, she buried her face in her hands. This was all too weird. Her head felt like it was spinning, and she was filled with an intense sense of loss, but she didn't know what for.

All four animals bounded over to her.

"Mia, it's a spell!"

Looking up, she saw that it was the fox speaking. He was staring at her intently with unusual indigo eyes.

"You can still get your memories back," said the wildcat. "Fight against the spell."

"You can do it, Mia," said the deer.

"We need you," said the squirrel, jumping onto her shoulder and smoothing her hair with his little paws. "Please try."

All of the animals were talking now! How strange this was.

"What memories?" said Mia. "I don't understand."

The fox put his
paws up on her legs.
She petted him. It was
strange—she felt as if she
knew him really well.
"Mia—magic is real," said
Lexi. "We're Star Friends."

"We've had a lot of adventures
together," added Violet. "We've fought
Shades and sent them back to the shadows.
Please believe us."

Mia looked into her green eyes. Violet did
usually tell the truth, and fuzzy memories were
starting to flash into her head of she and her
friends doing magic. She frowned.

"Mia," Sita said. "The other day, I promised
I'd never use magic on you, but I'm going to
break my promise. You made me believe in
my magic powers earlier today, and now I'm
going to make you do something—I'm going
to make you listen. Mia, you must believe us.

Magic *is* real."

More images formed in Mia's head. She and her friends in the clearing in the woods with the four animals…. She and Violet chasing after a gnome…. Trying to catch little yellow stretchy men with fangs….

"Magic *is* real?" she said slowly.

Bracken licked her. "Yes. Please believe."

She looked into his sparkling eyes, framed by his soft, rusty red fur, and felt the memories get stronger and more vivid. Crouching down, she hugged him, and breathing in his sweet smell, her confusion cleared like a fog lifting. "Of course magic is real!" she said. "I'm your Star Friend—you're my Star Animal!"

"Always," said Bracken, nuzzling into her.

"All the things I'm remembering—they really happened, didn't they?" Mia said, looking at the others.

"Yes!" Lexi, Violet, and Sita said together.

"It depends on what you're imagining, but I

presume so," said Sorrel dryly.

Mia felt a rush of love for all her friends and their animals. "Thank you for helping me," she said.

Bracken swung around and looked at Aunt Carol, who was still frozen, unable to move, her eyes flashing furiously. "And that's why Star Friends are better than people who use dark magic," he said triumphantly to her. "Star Friends and their animals trust and help each other—and when they do, they can defeat anything!"

Aunt Carol glared at him, still under the power of Sita's command to be silent.

"Where's the Dark Stone?" Mia said.

"I've got it," said Juniper.

Mia walked back to Aunt Carol. "Can you unfreeze her, Sita?"

"Are you sure?" Sita said.

"We've got to do something. We can't leave her frozen forever." Mia looked at Aunt Carol.

"We'll give you a chance. If we unfreeze you, you have to do what we say and promise never to use dark magic again." She glanced at Sita. "Unfreeze her."

Sita pointed at Aunt Carol. "You may move and speak."

"How dare you subdue me like that!" Aunt Carol hissed at Sita.

"Do you promise that you will never use dark magic again?" Mia said.

"No!" said Aunt Carol. Moving surprisingly quickly, she lunged for Juniper. He leaped away from her, keeping the stone safe.

"I command you to freeze!" cried Sita, pointing at her.

Aunt Carol froze once more.

"Face me," said Sita calmly. "And open your hands."

Aunt Carol did as she was told.

"Juniper, put the stone in Aunt Carol's hands," Sita said.

"What?" Mia, Lexi, and Violet exclaimed.

"Sita, what are you doing?" Willow said.

"It's the only thing we *can* do if we want to keep Westport safe," said Sita softly. "Aunt Carol, you will keep hold of the Dark Stone and say the spell to forget everything having to do with magic."

Aunt Carol tried to shake her head but couldn't. Only her eyes moved from side to side.

"Sita? Are you sure?" Lexi asked.

"It's using dark magic," said Juniper anxiously.

"It's making her use dark magic against herself," said Sita. She looked at them all steadily. "I really *am* sure this is the only way." Her voice rang with a new confidence. "We have to protect Westport."

"I agree with Sita," said Sorrel. The other animals nodded, too.

"Yes. Do it," Mia said.

"You may speak," said Sita to Aunt Carol.

"Others will come," Aunt Carol burst out in a rush. "You can stop me, but the town will not be safe. The clearing in the woods is a powerful magical place. You will face other threats more dangerous than me. You will—"

"Enough!" Sita commanded. "Say the spell that will make you forget! Say it now!"

Aunt Carol's mouth moved, and she looked like she was trying to keep it shut, but the harsh words burst out of her in a tangled stream.

The stone glowed for a moment, and then Aunt Carol's eyes clouded, and she looked around in confusion.

"It worked!" breathed Lexi.

"That was incredible, Sita," said Mia in awe.

"What's happening?" Aunt Carol said, looking dazed. "Why are we in my cellar?" She held out the Dark Stone. "And what's this?"

"That's mine," said Mia hurriedly, taking it
from her. The stone felt icy cold and seemed
to prickle her fingers. She shoved it in her
pocket. She saw Holly still hiding under the
table and had an idea. "We were here to help
you with the decorations, and then we heard
a noise down here—it was the Patels' missing
dog. I don't know how she got in here, but we
all came to get her and … then you banged
your head."

Aunt Carol blinked. "What about all these
other animals?"

The Star Animals vanished.

Aunt Carol blinked.

"What do you mean, Aunt Carol?" Mia
asked innocently.

Aunt Carol rubbed her eyes. "I thought I
saw wild animals…. My goodness, I really did
bang my head, didn't I?"

"You did. How about we go upstairs, and we
can make you a cup of tea?" Lexi said.

"I think that would be a good idea," said Aunt Carol faintly.

"And then we should take Holly home to the Patels," said Sita, crouching down and holding her hand out to the spaniel. "Come here, Holly. It's okay now. Come out."

Holly crept out, and Sita picked her up. The spaniel licked her face, immediately calming down as Sita petted and soothed her.

"The Christmas fair!" said Aunt Carol suddenly. "I need to take the decorations there."

"Don't worry. We'll take care of that for you," said Mia as they went upstairs. "You can rest and come to the fair later, when you're feeling better."

Aunt Carol smiled. "That's very kind of you, dears. Thank you very much."

15
TIME TO PLAY!

"What are we going to do about the decorations?" Mia whispered to the others when Aunt Carol was settled with a cup of tea. "We can't let them be sold at the fair."

"I have an idea," said Lexi. She turned to Aunt Carol and picked up one of the decorations. "Um, I think there might be a problem with these decorations."

"What kind of problem?" Aunt Carol said.

"It's the crystals in the center of the eyes. I showed the decoration you gave me to my mom, and she said it's a choking hazard for children."

Aunt Carol looked worried. "Oh, dear, I hadn't thought of that. I put them on because … because…." She frowned. "Well, I think I thought they looked pretty. Yes, that must be why."

"We could always take them off for you," said Lexi. "The decorations will look just as cute without the sparkly crystals."

"It really would be best," Violet added quickly as Aunt Carol hesitated.

"If you don't mind," said Aunt Carol. "It's a shame—but I would hate for a child to get hurt."

The four girls worked quickly. Soon, all of the crystals were sealed in a bag that Bracken buried deep in a flower bed in the yard, and the decorations were nothing more than just normal Christmas decorations.

"We'll take them to the town hall," said Sita. "And we'll take Holly home on the way."

They created a makeshift leash for Holly using a piece of thick ribbon from Aunt Carol's sewing box and then waved good-bye to Aunt Carol.

When they reached the Patels', the family was overjoyed to see Holly.

"Where did you find her?" Mrs. Patel asked as her two little girls hugged the spaniel in delight, and Holly bounded around them.

"In the woods," Mia said. They'd all decided that that would be the best story.

"Thank you so much for bringing her back," said Mrs. Patel.

"No problem!" the girls chorused.

The girls went to the town hall and delivered the decorations. Mia's mom was already there. "I'm very glad you're here, girls," she said. "We could use some extra help."

They were immediately swept up into getting the hall ready, the booths set up, and the coffee things arranged in the kitchen. At two o'clock, the hall doors were opened, and people flocked in. Soon, the whole place was full of people buying gifts, drinking tea and coffee, eating cakes, and chatting. The smell of gingerbread and cotton candy filled the air.

Mia's mom came up to her with Alex. He was wearing a Santa Claus hat and eating iced gingerbread. "The fair is going so well," said her mom happily. "Grandma Anne would be really happy to know that everything was continuing just as she would have wanted."

"Mmm-hmm," Mia said, glancing over at where Aunt Carol was selling her decorations. She had a feeling her grandma would be even more happy to know that they had managed to stop Aunt Carol's evil plans!

We'll have to keep a close eye on her in case the spell wears off, Mia thought. *And we need to think about what to do with the Dark Stone.*

"Do you want to buy some gingerbread to have with your friends?" her mom said. "Violet, Lexi, and Sita are over there." She got some money out of her purse.

"Thanks, Mom! Is it okay if we go for a walk?" Mia said.

"Sure. I'll see you back at home later."

Mia ran to join the others, and they bought slabs of warm gingerbread covered with sweet white icing and then headed for the clearing, munching happily. No one said a thing about what had happened with Aunt Carol. It was as though they all had a silent agreement not to speak about it until they reached the privacy of the clearing and could call their Star Animals.

They hurried down the track, past Grandma Anne's house with a "For Sale" sign up and along the overgrown footpath. Dark green ivy

scrambled through the holly bushes, with their
red berries providing splashes of color against all
the dull green and brown.

As they hurried into the clearing, the girls
called their animals' names, and the four Star
Animals appeared. Willow bucked joyfully,
Juniper raced up a tree, Sorrel rolled onto her
back in a patch of winter sunlight, and Bracken
chased his bushy tail.

"We did it!" said Sita, breathing a sigh of relief.

"Yep," said Violet. "Although we must remember to get rid of the decorations in our houses, too."

"And from my grandma's," said Sita.

Mia nodded. "Once we've gotten rid of them—and decided what to do with the Dark Stone—everyone will be safe."

"Until some new threat comes along," said Lexi. "Do you think Aunt Carol was right, and more evil will come here?"

"If it does, we'll stop it!" Violet declared.

"I'm sure you'll be able to, Violet," Sorrel said, weaving between her legs. "You saved the day today by turning into that Shade. And it was you who realized you could smash the globe."

Mia waited for Lexi to roll her eyes as she usually did when Sorrel boasted about Violet, but she didn't. She smiled and linked arms with Violet. "Sorrel's right—you were amazing, Violet."

"It wasn't just me," said Violet. "You were amazing when you snatched the Dark Stone, and Mia was amazing when she fought off the magic spell...."

"Only thanks to all of you," Mia put in.

"You were awesome, too, Sita," Violet went on. "If you hadn't commanded Aunt Carol, I don't know what would have happened."

Sita blushed. "I wouldn't have been able to do it without Mia. She made me realize why the magic wasn't working. I just had to believe."

Mia glanced around and remembered something Aunt Carol had said. "Is this clearing really powerful like Aunt Carol told us, Bracken? Will it attract other people wanting to do dark magic?"

"It might," said Bracken. "It's a crossing place—a place where the Star World and the human world meet. It contains a lot of power...."

"And power will always attract people who

want to use it for their own evil ends," said
Sorrel seriously. "We must all be on our guard."

"But those people aren't here yet," said
Juniper. "So for now, let's play!" He scampered
away and Lexi raced after him, using her magic
to climb a tree just as fast as him.

"Who wants to play a game of tag?" she
called, hanging down from a branch.

"Me!" said Violet to Mia's surprise. "Only if
I can shadow-travel though," she added with a
grin. "You're way too fast otherwise."

"Okay," said Lexi. "Catch me if you can!"
She swung through the branches before
dropping down to the clearing floor. She
landed in a patch of shadows and squealed as
Violet popped right up and tagged her.

"Got you!" Violet said, laughing.

Sita giggled. "One–nil Violet," she said, sitting
down on a tree stump and putting her arm over
Willow's back. "Willow and I will keep score!
We don't have a chance of keeping up with

you." Willow snuggled against her happily.

Bracken nestled into Mia's arms and licked her face.

"I'm so glad I didn't lose you today," she told him, remembering how awful she had felt when she thought she might never see him again.

He wriggled deeper into her arms. "I hated being stuck in that snow globe and not being able to get to you. I never want that to happen again."

Mia hugged him tightly. "It won't. We'll keep each other safe."

"Forever," Bracken promised. "Whatever comes."

Mia's heart swelled joyfully. She loved being able to do magic with Lexi,

Violet, and Sita, and being able to help and protect people, but most of all, she loved having Bracken as her Star Animal.

"I love you," she whispered to him.

He squirmed in delight and licked her nose.

"Come on, Mia!" shouted Lexi. "Come and play!"

Mia grinned at Bracken. "Should we join in?"

He nodded and jumped down from her arms. Bounding across the clearing, he leaped on top of Sorrel. "Time to play, pussycat!"

Sorrel yowled indignantly and sprang to her feet. Bracken tried to run away, but Sorrel was too fast. They rolled across the ground play-fighting while Willow shook her head and Juniper scampered around them excitedly.

Bursting with happiness, Mia ran to join her friends.

About the Author

Linda Chapman is the best-selling author of more than 200 books. The biggest compliment she can have is for a child to tell her he or she became a reader after reading one of her books. She lives in a cottage with a tower in Leicestershire, England, with her husband, three children, three dogs, and three ponies. When she's not writing, Linda likes to ride, read, and visit schools and libraries to talk to people about writing.

About the Illustrator

Lucy Fleming has been an avid doodler and bookworm since early childhood. Drawing always seemed like so much fun, but she never dreamed it could be a full-time job! She lives and works in a small town in England with her partner and a little black cat. When not at her desk, she likes nothing more than to be outdoors in the sunshine with a cup of hot tea.